Get ready to have more fun with gnomes! The 62 illustrations within this book feature the cheerful little creatures whooshing down ski slopes, relaxing on the beach, picking apples, strolling through farmers markets, and even celebrating holidays! Now the only thing they need is for you to fill their world with color. Relax, unwind, and live your best gnome life!

WHIMSICAL GNOMES

coloring book

Teresa Goodridge

DOVER PUBLICATIONS
Garden City, New York

Whimsical Gnomes Coloring Book, first published by Dover Publications in 2024, contains illustrations from *Creative Haven Garden Gnomes Coloring Book* and *Creative Haven Gnome for the Holidays Coloring Book*, both also originally published by Dover in 2024.

ISBN-13: 978-0-486-85251-5
ISBN-10: 0-486-85251-2

Publisher: Betina Cochran
Managing Editorial Supervisor: Susan Rattiner
Production Editor: Gregory Koutrouby
Cover Designer: Asya Blue
Creative Manager: Marie Zaczkiewicz
Interior Designer: Jennifer Becker
Production: Pam Weston, Tammi McKenna, Aysa Yilmaz

Manufactured in the United States of America
85251201   2024
www.doverpublications.com

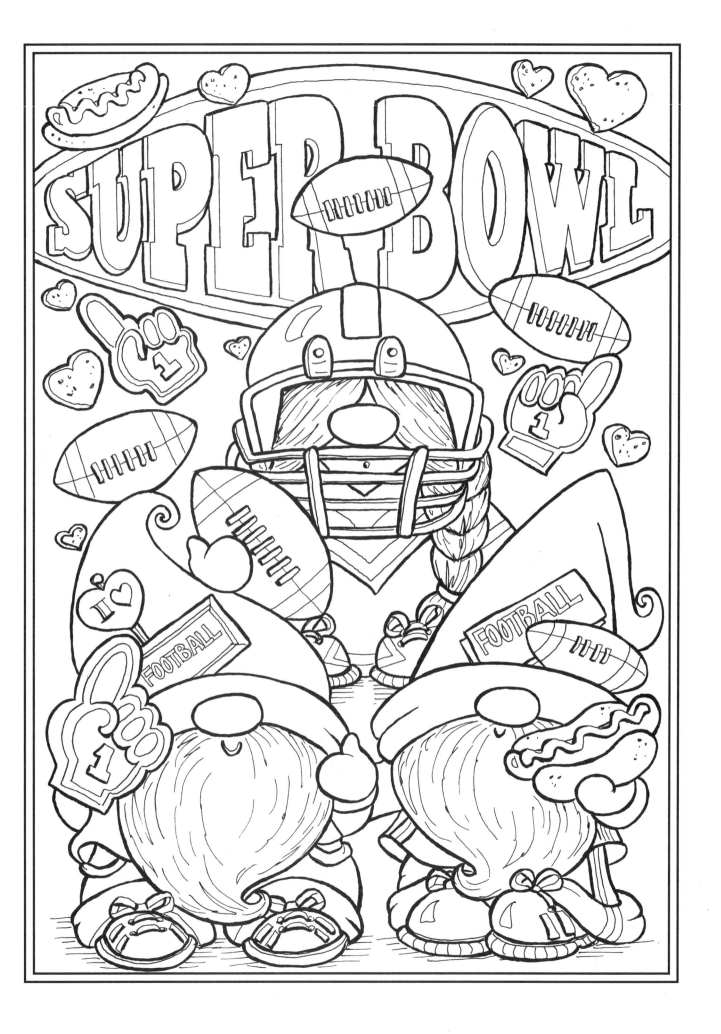

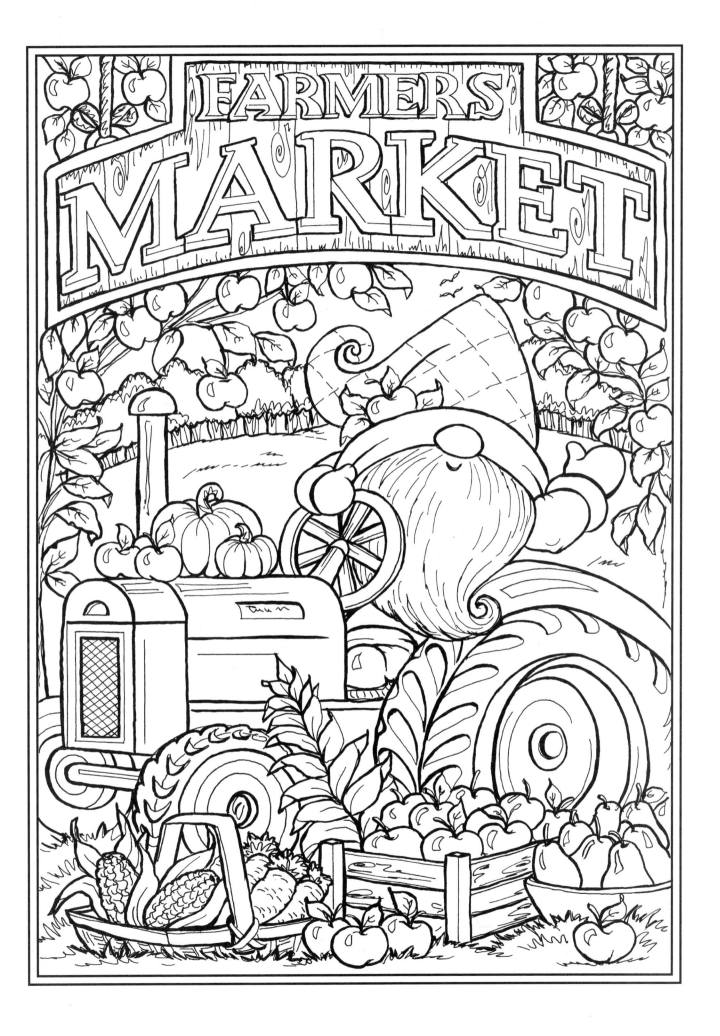